What to P

What to Put on for School?

By Cecilia Minden

2 What to put on for school?

I want to look my best at school. 3

4 I have a red top.

I will put on my red top.

6 I have tan pants.

I will put on my tan pants.

8 I have red socks.

I will put on my red socks.

I have a black belt.

I will put on my black belt.

12   I want to look my best at school.

This is what I will put
on for school.

Word List

sight words

a	is	on	want	school
for	like	put	What	
have	look	This	will	
I	my	to	put	

short a words

at
black
pants
tan

short e words

belt
best
red

short o words

socks
top

77 Words

What to put on for school?

I want to look my best at school.

I have a red top.

I will put on my red top.

I have tan pants.

I will put on my tan pants.

I have red socks.

I will put on my red socks.

I have a black belt.

I will put on my black belt.

I want to look my best at school.

This is what I will put on for school.

Published in the United States of America by Cherry Lake Publishing
Ann Arbor, Michigan
www.cherrylakepublishing.com

Photo Credits: © ayzek/Shutterstock.com, cover, 1, 15; © Ana Blazic Pavlovic/Shutterstock.com, back cover;
© baona/iStockphoto, 2; © monkeybusinessimages/Thinkstock.com, 3, 11, 13; © BLACKDAY/Shutterstock.com, 4;
© Monkey Business Images/Shutterstock.com, 5; © Olga Popova/Shutterstock.com, 6; © SergiyN/iStockphoto, 7;
© Madlen/Shutterstock.com, 8; © Africa Studio/Shutterstock.com, 9; © phoMAKER/Shutterstock.com, 10;
© Cynthia Farmer/Shutterstock.com, 12

Cherry Blossom Press is an imprint of Cherry Lake Publishing.

Library of Congress Cataloging-in-Publication Data has been filed and is available at catalog.loc.gov

Printed in the United States of America
Corporate Graphics

Cecilia Minden is the former director of the Language and Literacy Program at Harvard Graduate School of Education. She earned her PhD in Reading Education at the University of Virginia. Dr. Minden has written extensively for early readers. She is passionate about matching children to the very book they need to improve their skills and progress to a deeper understanding of all the wonder books can hold. Dr. Minden and her family live in McKinney, Texas.